50 THINGS YOU DIDN'T KNOW ABOUT

ANCIENT ROME

Written and Illustrated
by Sean O'Neill

RED CHAIR PRESS
Egremont, Massachusetts

50 Things You Didn't Know About is produced and published by Red Chair Press:
Red Chair Press LLC PO Box 333 South Egremont, MA 01258

LC record available at https://lccn.loc.gov/2019931710

First softcover edition ISBN: 978-1-63440-800-4

Printed in the United States of America

0822 2P CGS20

TABLE of CONTENTS

CHAPTER 1

THE REPUBLIC

Ancient Rome was a vast empire that dominated the classical world for over 1,000 years. The city of Rome was founded around 750 BCE but soon grew into an empire which, at its greatest, covered most of Europe, North Africa, and the Middle East—an area of over 2 million square miles. Although it eventually grew from a city to a powerful empire, in its early years, Rome was one of the world's first democracies. From the 5th century BCE until about 40 BCE, Rome was a republic where power was shared and citizens could vote.

1 The legendary founders of Rome were the brothers Romulus and Remus. According to the story, they were abandoned on a riverbank where they were discovered by a she-wolf, who fed them and cared for them. The image of the two baby boys nursing from the wolf is still a popular symbol of Rome, and is even the emblem of the AC Roma soccer team.

2 In the earliest days of Rome, the city was ruled by a succession of kings. The last king, Tarquin II, was overthrown, and the Roman Republic was created in 509 BCE.

3 By the middle of the 1st century BCE, the city of Rome had more than a million inhabitants.

4 In early Rome it was illegal to bury gold along with the body of a dead person, with one exception—gold teeth were allowed into the grave.

5 The English word **"candidate"** comes from the Latin* *candidatus*, which means "whitened," and refers to the specially bleached togas that politicians wore during campaigns.

6 During the period of the republic, Rome was ruled by a **senate** made up of 600 members. The word "senate" comes from the Latin word *senex* which means "old man."

*Latin was the language of Ancient Rome.

7 Speaking of whitening, a popular method of bleaching clothes was to soak them in urine. The natural ammonia had a whitening effect on garments—and that's not all. Romans also used urine to whiten their teeth! Blech!

8 During a period of unrest before the establishment of the Empire, the Roman statesman Cicero was killed. His head and right hand were nailed up in the center of Rome as a warning to other would-be rebels.

9 Julius Caesar, the most famous leader in Roman history, was not actually an **emperor**. He was a very popular and powerful military leader, but when he tried to seize more power, the Senate assassinated him on March 15, 44 BCE. This date is now remembered as "the Ides of March."

10 In addition to words such as *senate* and *palace*, Ancient Rome gave us some common catchphrases, such as "beware Greeks bearing gifts," and "fiddling while Rome burns."

11 Leadership of the senate was shared between two people called Consuls. Consuls were accompanied everywhere they went by officials called lictors, who carried a bundle of sticks and an axe, and could be ordered to beat or kill a citizen on command.

CHAPTER 2

WARFARE & EMPIRE

The city of Rome extended its influence around the Mediterranean through the power of the largest and strongest army in the ancient world. The military soon became the most influential part of society. As the empire grew in size, political power shifted away from the senate to a more centralized, individual leader—the emperor.

12 In 390 BCE soldiers from Gaul (today's France) were preparing an early attack on Rome's Capitoline Hill, but it was saved when Roman soldiers were awakened by honking geese.

13 The Romans fought three wars, called the Punic Wars, against Carthage in North Africa. In 218 BCE, Carthaginian general Hannibal famously crossed the Alps mountain range riding 37 elephants. Hannibal's army was eventually defeated and they lost 14,000 men.

14 The longest sustained period of warfare in human history was a series of wars between the Romans and the Persians. The conflict went on for over 700 years!

15 Roman soldiers were divided into legions of 5,000 soldiers, called *legionaries*. By the 2nd century CE the Roman army had 150,000 legionaries.

16 One weapon in the legionaries' **arsenal** was a wooden javelin. It was thrown at the enemy, and was designed to break on impact so an enemy soldier couldn't throw it back.

17 Roman soldiers advanced on their enemies by surrounding themselves in a "shell" made by their shields, which they called a "tortoise."

18 The Roman Empire reached its greatest size under emperor Hadrian. When he got to northern Britain, he decided he'd gone far enough, and built a wall 75 miles long to keep out Scottish tribes. Hadrian's wall still stands today.

19 The first actual Emperor of Rome was Julius Caesar's adopted son, Octavian, who was given the name Augustus when he became emperor. Emperors would rule Rome for the next 400 years.

20 The phrase "fiddling while Rome burns" refers to the Emperor Nero, who, according to legend, sang and played the fiddle while the city burned in the Great Fire of Rome. There's only one problem with this story: the fiddle wasn't invented until many centuries later!

21 Many Roman emperors believed they could gain immunity from poisoning by taking a small amount of every known poison every day. The poison mixture was known as the Mithridatium.

22 One of the craziest emperors ever was Caligula, who ruled from 37 to 41 CE. Caligula was infamous for odd behavior. He once ordered a legion of soldiers to collect seashells along the beach, and even tried to have his favorite horse made a senator! Like many other unpopular emperors, Caligula was eventually killed by his own men.

23 An emperor named Valerian was taken prisoner during the long war against Persia. While a prisoner, the Persian king used him as a step to mount his horse!

CHAPTER 3

THE ARENA

Probably the most familiar image of Ancient Rome is the bloody spectacle of two gladiators viciously fighting to the death in front of a stadium full of screaming fans. While there is some truth to this version, it's not the whole story. Some of the more unusual facts about competition in classical Rome may surprise you.

24 The greatest arena in Rome was the Colosseum. It was opened in 80 CE and could hold 50,000 spectators. During gladiator contests, the floor of the Colosseum was covered in sand to soak up all the blood!

25 Competition in the arena was not always to the death. A defeated gladiator could appeal for mercy. The emperor would listen to the opinion of the crowd, and then make his judgment with a thumbs-up or thumbs-down.

26 Although dangerous, fighting as a gladiator was a glamorous profession. One emperor named Commodus even entered the arena to fight. Commodus was a bit of an oddball. He once tried to re-name Rome after himself. Eventually, he, too, was killed by his own generals.

27 Gladiators were popular heroes, like today's sports or movie stars. Graffiti found at the site of Pompeii reads: "Celadus the Thracian makes all the girls sigh."

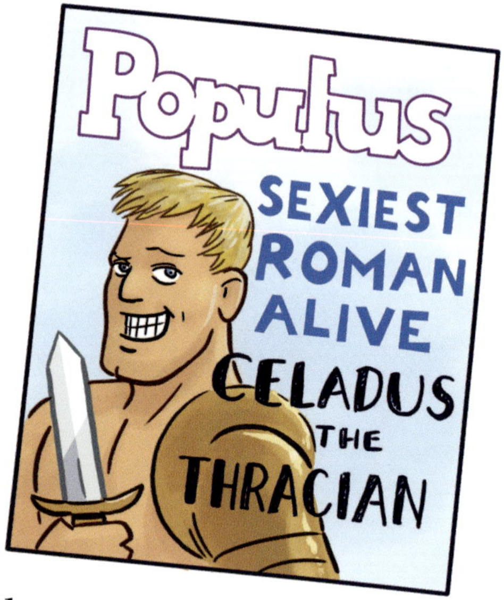

28 Before the gladiators entered the ring, crowds were entertained by the spectacle of wild animals such as tigers and bears devouring each other or being stalked and killed by "huntsmen."

29 Gladiators prepared for the arena at a training school called the Ludus Magnus just outside the Colosseum.

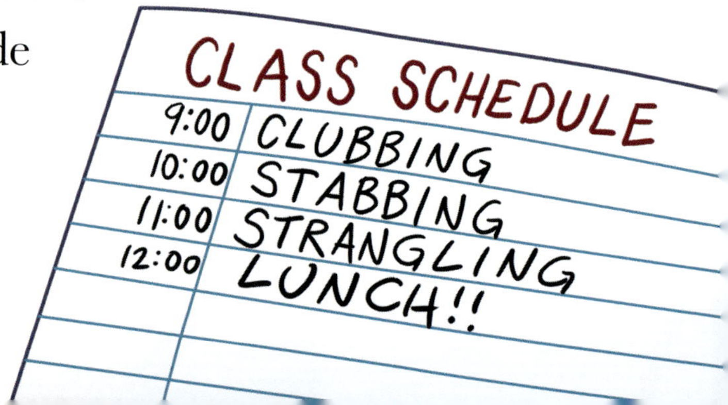

30 The largest tournament ever held was in the year 107 CE. It featured 5,000 pairs of gladiators doing battle in one day!

31 Gladiators that won their freedom were given a wooden sword, which symbolized the fact that they would never have to fight in the arena again.

32 One type of gladiator was called a "blind-fighter." They were put in a helmet that completely covered their faces and entered the ring with another "blind-fighter." They each had to feel around for their opponent until they bumped into each other.

33 The bloody battles between gladiators were not the favorite sport in Rome. Chariot races were much more popular. Roman chariots were pulled by teams of two or four horses, and races were between four teams: the Blues, Greens, Reds, and Whites.

34 A Charioteer named Pompeius Musclosus who raced for the Blues racked up over 3,500 wins!

35 The largest racing arena in the empire was the Circus Maximus in Rome. It was 570 meters long and held 250,000 people! In the races, 12 chariots would race each other over a distance of 5 miles (8 km).

36 Chariot racing wasn't as dangerous as being a gladiator, but there were many crashes and collisions. It was worth the risk, though—winners were given… a palm leaf. Hmm, on second thought…

CHAPTER 4

DAILY LIFE

Ancient Rome was one of the world's earliest examples of a highly organized and complex society. Because of the large size of the empire, many laws and codes of behavior were established to unite people of many cultures as Roman citizens. While they may not be quite as exciting as the battles of gladiators and legionaries, many details of everyday life are still pretty unusual.

37 A lot of what we know about Roman daily life comes from **excavations** at the sites of Pompeii and Herculaneum. On August 24, 79 CE, a volcano called Mount Vesuvius erupted, burying the two cities in 60 feet (18 m) of boiling mud. This preserved many artifacts for future generations to discover.

38 A marketplace in Rome called Trajan's Markets featured 150 shopping stalls arranged in a three-story structure—history's first shopping mall!

39 You had to be careful walking around the streets of Rome. It was very common to be hit by someone dropping garbage from an apartment window above. Or worse—emptying their toilet pot!

40 Because Roman homes were lit by oil lamps and heated with fireplaces, the risk of fire was high. The first emperor, Augustus created the first fire department, called the "Watchmen." They were a group of slaves trained to put out fires.

41 Romans had very exotic tastes when it came to food. One elaborate dish included fish livers, peacock and pheasant brains, and, a particular favorite: flamingo tongues.

42 Romans ate an early style of pizza called *offelae*. It was similar to our pizza with one major difference—no tomato sauce. (Tomatoes weren't brought to Europe until the 16th century).

43 Ancient Romans kept clean together in large public baths. They didn't have soap, so they would rub their skin with olive oil and scrape off dirt and dead skin with a scraping tool called a *strigil.*

44 Dead skin cells were usually washed away—unless they were from a gladiator. Sweat and skin scrapings from gladiators were put into bottles and sold to women as a facial cream!

45 Roman households didn't have soap. Dirty dishes were cleaned by scrubbing them with sand and then rinsing in water.

46 Using Roman toilets was dangerous business. Creatures living in the sewage system were prone to crawling up and biting unsuspecting toilet users.

CHAPTER 5

RELIGION & MYTHS

Ancient Roman gods did not have stories and myths as colorful as their Greek counterparts, but some of these facts about the habits and beliefs of Romans may seem equally as outlandish and unusual.

47 Romans had their own pantheon of gods, although they "borrowed" several of them from ancient Greece and just gave them different names. Many of those names will be very familiar—Mercury, Venus, Mars, Jupiter, Saturn, and Neptune—that's where we get the names of most of the planets in our solar system.

48 Most Roman homes had shrines to the gods. One god that many citizens believed would protect their homes was a spirit in the form of a bearded snake.

49 Our calendar was created by the Romans, and several of our months are named after their gods. June for Juno, May for Maia, and March was named after Mars, god of war, because springtime was when the fighting could start again after taking a break for winter.

50 The Roman goddess Ceres was the goddess of grain and the harvest. It's where we get our word "cereal."

Glossary

arsenal: a collection of weapons

candidate: someone who runs for election to a position of honor

emperor: the one (male) who rules an Empire

excavation: the process of digging up some place

senate: a powerful group of men who made laws and helped rule the Republic and Roman Empire

Explore Rome More

Books

Benoit, Peter. *Ancient Rome*. Scholastic, 2012.

Hawes, Alison. *A Roman Soldier's Handbook*. Crabtree, 2010.

James, Simon. *Ancient Rome(DK Eyewitness Books)*. DK Children's Publishing, 2015.

Malam, John. *You Wouldn't Want to be a Roman Gladiator!* Franklin Watts, rev. ed 2012.

Medina, Nico. *Who Was Julius Caesar?* Grosset & Dunlap, 2014.

On the Web

National Geographic: Ten Facts About Ancient Rome
https://www.natgeokids.com/nz/discover/history/romans/10-facts-about-the-ancient-romans/

Index

About the Author/Illustrator

Sean O'Neill is an illustrator and writer living in Chicago. He is the creator of the *Rocket Robinson* series of graphic novels. Sean loves history, trivia, and drawing cartoons, so this project is pretty much a dream assignment. And it comes with Romans on toilets!